A Changing

of the Heart

Also by Kris Radish

Fiction:

The Elegant Gathering of White Snows

Dancing Naked at the Edge of Dawn

Annie Freeman's Fabulous Traveling Funeral

Searching for Paradise in Parker P.A.

The Sunday List of Dreams

The Shortest Distance Between Two Women

Hearts on a String

Tuesday Night Miracles

A Grand Day to Get Lost

The Year of Necessary Lies

A Dangerous Woman From Nowhere

The Tender Resurrection of Bold Women

Non-Fiction:

Run, Bambi, Run: The Beautiful Ex-Cop and Convicted Murderer Who Escaped to Freedom and Won America's Heart

The Birth Order Effect: How to Better Understand Yourself and Others

Gravel on the Side of the Road–True Stories From a Broad Who Has Been There

A Changing of the Heart

The Tale of the Hummingbird
and the Goose

K.A. RADISH

Bestselling Author of Annie Freeman's
Fabulous Traveling Funeral

HUMMING
WORDS
BOOKS

INTRODUCTION

I WROTE THIS tiny book 30 years ago when my children were babies. This story flew out of my own heart, a wild bird that landed on these pages, as a way for my son and daughter to learn about what is truly important in life.

If there was ever a time to talk about kindness, friendship, sacrifice, love, and courage, it is now.

This isn't just a book for children but a story that should also make you remember what is really important. Just think, if the birds can do it, so can I!

I really believe animals, especially birds, have souls. How can you not be filled with the wonder of creation and life when you see a Hummingbird, a Goose, a Cardinal, any bird at all, dancing toward the clouds, where I know the Great Bird Gods are whispering to them.

We can hear whispers from up there too. But we must pause to listen and open our hearts.

Be kind. We are all neighbors and part of one amazing human family.

Always,

Kris Radish

A Changing of the Heart

Legend has it that tiny hummingbirds sometimes lodge themselves behind the wings of majestic geese during migration.

Native Americans tell the story often and they know the secrets of the sky are always visible to those with open hearts.

1

IT WAS A DAY for high sailing.

The tiny Hummingbird, his fragile wings rustling in the fast air, decided this was a day to fly higher than he ever had before. It was early fall and the air, even high up, was still warm, still soothing to the body of a bird that weighed only a feather more than the wind it sailed on.

He played in the wind for a while, letting it drift across his back through his magnificent colors, and over his feathery wings. When the currents moved through his thimble-light head in short, gusty, waves the small bird knew that it was time to challenge the sky. This was the day for him to soar out of the sight of earth, higher maybe than any bird had ever soared, beyond the limits others had set for him.

The bird was alone. He was one of the most beautiful Hummingbirds in the area and his good looks set him apart from the rest. Many other birds, impressed by his stunning colors, thought he was aloof. Indeed, the bird was a beauty. His red head and crown were of a color no other birds had ever seen and his fellow birds thought he was magical. His neck was bright pink, his chest many beautiful shades of blue, and when the Hummingbird moved through the air the green purple feathers on his back made him look like a swift blur of color.

This wonderful bird was usually seen alone, but other birds who dared to fly with him soon found out he was a gentle spirit given to moments of playfulness, and even more moments of simple, kind, genuine companionship.

The few birds who came to know him through adventures of the sky always described him as a calm and serious flyer, a bird to be counted on, despite all those long moments of silence when birds must simply focus on riding the unseen winds. Even those who didn't know him well remembered the summer the Hummingbird befriended a lost female bird from far in the South and they had become inseparable. Indeed, the Hummingbird had fallen in love with the lost beauty.

Rumors were running almost as wild as the low air currents that year and everyone was surprised when his love disappeared late the following spring. Suddenly, just as before, the Hummingbird was alone again, his colors shining against the soon-to-be summer sky, and no one had the courage to ask what had become of his companion.

After that, those who watched the Hummingbird noticed he seemed to be more daring and adventurous than anyone had ever remembered. He would be gone for days at a time and his return to the sky brought a sigh of relief to those who had grown accustomed to his bright wings flashing above them.

It seemed that each season drove him higher and higher into the endless sky.

"Look, look," the birds would say as the Hummingbird, streaking with color, whirled almost straight up toward the clouds. It was as if some magical and unseen force was pushing him.

Some tried to follow but not many had the courage to challenge the tricky winds that danced close to the clouds. The Hummingbird, like other birds of his kind, really was as light as a feather. In fact, he was the lightest of all birds that flew through the air. It was the quick flap, flap, flapping of the tiny wings that gave him his strength. But the source of his courage, of his motivations, and sense of adventure... the source of that no one knew for certain.

So, it was no surprise that fall day when other Hummingbirds watched the bright colored bird disappear into the cloudless sky. Up and up he went, higher than ever, lost in the thrills of the excitement of his freedom. He circled the birds watching below him. Smiling, he nodded his fine red head, and he was gone.

Once he lost sight of his companions the small bird drifted into his own private world. His mind was quick to wander in the thin high air and as always, his thoughts turned to his lost friend, the one bird he had dared to love, and claim as his mate.

"What a beauty she was," the Hummingbird said, aching with the memory. "Where are you, where are you?" he called to no one but the wind and to nothing but that long, high sky.

He closed his eyes for a moment. In that second, lost in her memory, forgetting his place, forgetting the trickery of high winds that were unfamiliar to him, he suddenly lost control.

At first it was just a slight push from the air around him that brought the Hummingbird back from his thoughts. But the second gust of air brought him a strong feeling of fright and the third gust a terrifying feeling of remembering something very important

From the time he was a small bird, training for the winds of life with his family in the low desert lands of the west, he had been warned of the fall weather.

"Never soar high when the moon hangs low and when you see it shadowed and glowing," his father had told him. "There is bad magic in those winds, and if you are not careful you will be swept away forever."

His father had told him of a young Hummingbird who simply disappeared one night. His family waited and waited. They watched the bright clouds dim and then darken. They called for him endlessly into the night and soon their calls were sounds of grief and they cried far into the next day. The bird was gone, trapped by the smiling and mischievous sky, by the fall wind that warms, and then without warning sucks you into itself, claiming you for its own.

Somehow the young Hummingbird was remembering all this as he flipped end over end in another fall sky. Even with his strength the Hummingbird was no match for the angry wind. He tried to control his wings, to master his flight pattern, and move himself to a place of safety.

But the more he struggled, the more painful his fumbling flight became. Already he could feel the ache of the fierce wind on his thread-thin bones, and already he knew he had made a terrible, terrible mistake. Over and over he tumbled, thinking of nothing then but only of each movement, each breath he took. In almost that same moment he let go of the control of his wings, tucked his battered head into his now frail chest, and succumbed to the sky. His only comfort was the last ounce of warmth from his own body and another older thought.

It was a thought of his beloved mother. The bird wondered where she was and what she was doing. The wind continued to push him east, faster than he could ever have dared to travel on his own.

"Oh, mother," the Hummingbird said softly to himself. "I remember you. Everything about you was kind. If you were here now, I would feel safe. I would feel warm. I would not be frightened."

For a time just the mere thought of his mother did warm him, and perhaps it was that thought that kept him aloft during his uncontrolled ride through the clouds. But then the sky became thick with dense clouds and the ride became rougher and the clouds even darker.

The Hummingbird was tired beyond anything he had ever known before. His struggling had made him hungry and he desperately wanted water. His wish now was only to break through one cloud and descend slowly to the ground below to something or someone familiar. He ached from his bones to his heart and from his heart to his soul.

He cried once. His sobs of pain turned into sobs of sudden anguish for what he might miss if he were to die in that sky–a sky that had once, and almost forever, given him so much happiness, and so much solace. He cried for lost love. What joy and love the other Hummingbird had brought him, and then what sadness when she had left. After that not even the challenge of the high winds could comfort him, and he pushed on and on looking for something to fill his empty space. He cried again and again for missing her. He cried for missing his friends— silent as they might be and silent as he might be. Friends who watched him nurse his ache of lost love and who never questioned his comings and goings. He cried because he was lost, because he had made a terrible mistake, because he had abandoned the teachings of a lifetime. He cried for his bruised and battered body and still he was carried farther and farther by the Master Wind.

The Hummingbird lost consciousness after that. The winds were kinder to him then, tossing and tumbling his fragile body from one cloud to another. The day passed and the night air was cold in the fast-moving space. But even that did not wake the Hummingbird. He slept uncontrollably until the sky was hazy white, until today was tomorrow, until his world seemed like nothing but a bad nightmare.

He floated through the early morning, dreaming the dreams of the sick and sorry, the dreams of those who might never awaken, those who might never see another white, hazy morning, and feel the warm sun on cold morning wings.

Toward the middle of the second day, still trapped in the changing of the season's wind, the clouds and sky had a change of heart. They released their hold on the Hummingbird. It was a sudden decision by nature's forces, a decision usually not made so quickly, and usually not in favor of a mistaken bird. When those forces let the Hummingbird go it was with one quick and smooth movement.

The bruised bird never woke up as he drifted downward. If he had been awake he would have been amazed at the height he had attained. He was so high, that it seemed like minutes before the Hummingbird passed through normal layers of clouds— the layers birds who are considered daring fly to. But the Hummingbird was way beyond that point and he paid dearly for his mistake.

The wind carried him on a gentle current to the cold earth below. It was an unfamiliar place for a bird from the West. There were no mountains. No dry desert winds. There was only cold, and in the middle of that great Midwestern cornfield the fragile bird drifted down safely. After that the forgiving winds only stayed a moment. They were gone in a flash, gone before anyone or anything could see that quick moment of kindness. Then the bruised and battered Hummingbird was all alone.

Hours passed and the bird lay still. The field around him was huge and spread out across the rolling hills in an endless line of precision. The stalks of corn, long since barren of the year's harvest, looked like rows of tired soldiers resting for the next season. It was a stark and terrifying scene.

2

WHEN THE HUMMINGBIRD did awaken, it was with a sudden start, as if one of those corn soldiers had pushed him. In that brief moment of awakening the bird forgot for a few seconds about his painfully battered body, about his wild daring run into the sky, about his hellish ride through the winds. For a second he was free of pain.

He lay there surrounded by unfamiliarity, and then for a second time in just a few days, he was totally terrified. The smell of the air was different— so damp he could almost feel what he was smelling. It wasn't the dry, crisp, scent of the desert. Looking up he could see no mountains, only bluish sky, speckled with tiny white clouds, the clouds that often appear after a fierce storm. He had no idea where he was or what would happen to him.

It was difficult for the tiny Hummingbird to move. "Look at me," the bird cried to himself, "I am going to die... I am going to die."

At the moment his death was a possibility. The beautiful bird was ripped and torn, and his once bright colors were coated with the dark brown mud of the cornfield. Beyond the loss of his physical powers the bird had lost something even more important in his wild ride through the sky. He had lost his will to live and his physical pain made him slip closer and closer to death. Once he tried to move his wings, tried to make some part of his body come alive, but with his inner and outer strength all but gone, his body and spirit were almost lifeless.

"I am so thirsty," he cried. "If I could only get a drink."

His voice trailed off; a voice so small in the middle of all that surrounded him. There was no one to hear the Hummingbird. He was totally alone in the unfamiliar field. Hundreds of miles away from his home and from everything that meant life and safety to him.

The Hummingbird fell asleep again and how long he slept he will never remember. When he woke again, the day and another night had passed. Morning was breaking bright and clear through the downed cornstalks.

By then the tiny bird was desperately ill and there was no reason at all for any life to be in his body. Indeed, he wanted to die, and he would die unless something saved him... something like a miracle.

He had given up struggling. He lay still, his mind dragging along, thinking about nothing and everything. His thoughts were jumping over each other in a random cruise of abandon. His wings seemed damaged beyond repair, and it only seemed a matter of time before the beautiful bird would die... so alone and so ill in the huge field.

3

THE GOOSE SPOTTED the Hummingbird long before anyone else did. Others had flown over the small bird, but it took a Goose with a keen eye, a Goose who was always watching, always ready to see, the tiny, colored bird body far below.

The huge bird had been flying over the big cornfield for several days with his family and friends. The Geese searched for leftover bits and pieces of corn from the recent fall harvest. Even when the harvest was bad, and the kernels few, the gentleman farmer who owned the land always found something to leave out for the Geese. How he loved to hear them honk, honk, honking as they flew toward his house. The Goose liked the big friendly man who always waved at them, smiling into the sun, and calling out a cheerful greeting.

The farmer had been a friend of the birds for years and years, and when the winter snows came early or the spring rains ruined the miles and miles of corn, the geese knew they could always find food from the Gentleman farmer. Few geese, however, were as grateful as the Goose who spotted the Hummingbird.

The huge flock of geese had been lingering near the farmer's field now for over a week. They were busy loading up on sweet pieces of corn before the long trip south.

It was almost time to take that dangerous, tiring, and very long trip. It was a trip that would bring them out of the grey skies of winter to the blue skies of the cold season in a warmer place.

The huge storm that carried the Hummingbird to that same field came as no surprise to the Goose. He had felt it coming before the sky darkened, and when it finally hit with all the fierceness of any change of the season storm, the bird was ready.

"Winter, winter," is what the other birds mumbled when the pelting storm hit them.

They knew it was the time to move on to the blue skies waiting for them so far away. Nature would only warn them once. They must leave soon.

The good-natured Goose wasn't angered by the cold winds. He knew it was time to leave the rolling hills and forests behind for another season. Time to leave the smiling farmer and his plentiful fields. Time to fly over the big, blue lake where the waters are so clear you can scare yourself flying so low, bumping along with your own reflection, as if you have a twin.

No one really looked forward to the big fly. Sometimes birds would fall out of the line never to be seen again. Others would simply not try, and their winters were spent cold and alone. For years the Goose tried to persuade others to drop down and help those birds in distress. His words were never taken seriously as he flew with the others, and the Goose never had the courage to fly ahead and ask the leaders for permission to help his brother and sister birds. Instead, he had always flown on, the wind in his eyes, his heart aching with a longing to help and embarrassment at his own lack of courage.

Now the geese could begin leaving for the big fly at any moment. The leaders were meeting the day after the storm to decide when to go. Most of the birds were strong. Most were ready, fat with corn for the endless, endless, endless journey of the fly south. The Goose, too, was ready and he knew from the past that the group would probably leave after one more feeding.

The Goose was not the largest in the flock, but he was a strong bird. His feathers did not stand out, and most of the other birds considered him to be simple and plain. But beyond those drab feathers there was something that had already made the Goose special and set him apart.

The other geese picked on him constantly because he was always so eager to help the other birds. Despite his lack of courage in the sky, the Goose was always willing to help birds in distress. Usually they were younger birds, left by their families to survive in a world where no bird should be alone. But this was the custom of the flock and a way to weed out the weak from the strong.

"Look at you, look at you," the other birds would call to him, laughter filling up their throats as he worked day after day to teach an abandoned or weak bird the tricks of survival.

"Their mothers don't want them, and you do," they would taunt as they flew squawk, squawk, squawking past him.

The Goose pretended not to hear them. He didn't know why he was different from the other birds. He didn't know or understand why he had such an endless desire to help. Surely, with his years of experience he could have become one of the flock leaders by now. He was strong and it was a strength he had been born with.

When he was born his family thought they had a new leader, a bird they could be proud of, a bird that would stand apart. But as the Goose grew, his father began to call him a dreamer. He was told over and over again that he would be nothing more than a simple follower.

"A bird has to be hard," his father told him. "To survive you must first think of yourself and then of the others. "To be a great leader you must teach this and other ways of the skies to the birds and they will follow you and you will gain their respect."

From as far back as he could remember though, the Goose never cared about being a leader. He perfected his flying and his hunting and survival skills until he was one of the best. But his heart was not in the harsh and sometimes selfish skills needed to be a leader, and his father, disgusted, finally left the Goose to his own ways, to his own life.

That is why the Goose spotted the Hummingbird in that cold, dark cornfield. The Goose, who had trained himself to have a keen eye, circled the Hummingbird once, twice, three times before he got low enough to see what the bright color was all about. When the Goose discovered the Hummingbird, he was shocked to see such a tiny bird there in the middle of the cornfield so late in the season. He flew very low over the small bird for the fourth time and landed close enough to get a good look at him.

What the Goose saw made his kind heart sink. The lifeless body of the battered Hummingbird lay crumpled against the cornstalk, and the Goose thought for sure the tiny bird was dead. He moved closer, and it was then that the tiny bird stirred, waking for a brief moment from his troubled and painful sleep.

At first the once-beautiful bird did not see the huge Goose standing near him. His vision was blurred, and he was surprised and disappointed to see that he was still alive. With his thoughts still drifting like the endless fall winds, the little bird tried to focus his eyes. When he did, he saw the huge Goose standing close and staring at him.

"Please, please help me," the Hummingbird cried, for a moment forgetting his wish to die.

The cry startled the Goose and at the same time touched him with the same kind of compassion he had felt for other helpless birds. It was obvious that the small bird was hurt badly. The Goose wondered where the bird had come from and knew for certain that he had gotten trapped in the wild arms of the storm. The Goose inched closer, not sure what he was afraid of, yet daring to say nothing.

After his cry for help the Hummingbird lay still. His eyes were closed tightly, and his tiny beak was stretched open and pointing at the sky.

The Goose closed in on the Hummingbird then and he could immediately detect the sickly smell that he often sensed around other weak birds. Perhaps it was the smell of death, the Goose did not know. But the smell, the sight of the tiny bird lying there so still, so helpless, moved the big Goose. Very gently and very carefully he pressed his beak into the Hummingbird's small head.

Feeling the faint movement of life, the Goose knew the Hummingbird was alive. He also knew that every second mattered and that the small bird needed water as soon as possible.

Almost on instinct the large bird's wings picked him off the ground and carried him low and fast to the nearby stream. The Goose filled his mouth with water and in a matter of seconds he was back beside the Hummingbird.

This time he dropped down by the bird without hesitation, and with his long swooping neck he pushed the Hummingbird so he could reach his mouth. The Hummingbird never moved on his own, but in his deep sleep he dreamt he was drinking from one of the many desert pools back home, and he swallowed every drop of water the Goose gave him.

Without another thought the Goose went back for more water and again the Hummingbird drank. The Goose was relieved to know he was helping the small bird and he flew back for water again. On his last trip he began thinking about where the Hummingbird might be from.

"His colors, even tarnished, are a color I have never seen," the Goose thought. "I wonder where his home is, what he is like and tonight, when the cold air comes, what in the world will I do with him?"

The Goose was torn by his last thought. It was a thought he'd had before when dealing with other birds from his own flock. Could he take the death of one more weak bird without doing or saying something? Could his heart stand to watch another bird drop from the sky, even a bird as foreign, as tiny, as misplaced as this Hummingbird?

For a moment the Goose simply did not know. His mind was racing with emotions. His heart was beating fast in his chest and he was filled with a sudden overwhelming wave of sadness. Desperate to know what to do, he prayed to the Great Goose God. The God who gives all birds their strength, their ability to soar on the back of the sightless wind. The God who at birth gives each bird the important feelings and instincts of survival and longing for life.

And it was the same Great Goose God who said:

"All those creatures soaring through the air should feel a common bond and a kinship of spirit, for you alone are the creatures whose souls extend to your wings. You alone know the joy of total freedom as you fly close to my heavens. And you shall use your gift of life, your great gift of flying freedom with all those you see, all those you touch."

"Oh, Great God, help me," cried the Goose, stretching his neck back across his own body. "Help me be strong, help me share my strength no matter the cost, no matter who makes fun of me, no matter how I might have to suffer."

The Great Goose God watched the Goose stretched out in the fall field, and as is the ways of Gods, he had pity on him. He was fond of the Goose, for in his own quiet way the Goose had proven time and time again that the gift of life can be passed on. The God had watched year after year as the other geese had tormented the Goose, calling him weak because he liked to help the other birds. It was with that remembering that the Great Goose God bestowed on the Goose a gift of courage, a gift of sudden strength, and a gift of forgiveness and understanding.

The gifts passed from the God to the Goose with a sudden surge of swift light. It was a light that is imperceptible, a light that cannot be felt, even by the receiver of the gift.

And with the light the Great God blew these words of caution into the soul of the Goose.

"It will never be easy, even with this new courage, this new strength. Remember me, I will always be with you as you soar higher than you ever dreamed."

The Goose finished his prayer in the field, not knowing even then that God had already looked kindly upon him. For a time, he did not even feel or realize the sudden change in himself.

The sky was beginning to darken then and the other geese had long since left the area for the night with a decision made to leave the next day for the south. The Goose ate as quickly as possible, knowing he would need all the strength he could gather for what he was about to do.

When he finished eating, he flew back to the Hummingbird. He hovered over the small bird. The difference in their sizes was striking. The Goose could have crushed the Hummingbird with one, swift movement. He finally landed next to the slight bird and with his great and powerful wings he covered the Hummingbird with his warmth, with his new gift of courage and with the gift of kindness that he had always possessed. He was ready to stay with the Hummingbird through the night, warming him so the little bird might live to see another day.

The Goose tucked his own head inside his big, downy chest and within a few minutes he slept the peaceful sleep of someone who is totally content. The warmth kept the Hummingbird from waking up and already the tattered bird was beginning to heal.

The night was cold and there is no doubt the little bird would never have made it through without the big Goose to warm him. The chilling cold that followed, along with the huge storm that had dropped the Hummingbird into the cornfield, had lingered especially long in the valley, and a thick frost covered the Goose and everything in sight that was exposed to the night air. The thick fluffy feathers of the Goose were like a warm blanket on the Hummingbird. He slept warm and safe through the night, never knowing it was the Goose who was giving him back his life.

It was early morning before the Goose ruffled his feathers and woke from his deep sleep. He uncovered the Hummingbird and was surprised to see the small bird stirring.

The Hummingbird came awake slowly. He had no idea where he was or even who he was for a few moments. The events of the past few days were hazy in his mind. Then when he looked up, he was startled and frightened to see the large Goose hovering over him. While the Hummingbird had seen geese before, flying and honking off in the distance, he had never been this close to such a large bird. The size of the Goose was frightening.

The Goose sensed this and spoke quickly.

"Don't be afraid little Hummingbird," he said softly. "You are very sick and in a place that must be far from your home. You are safe with me."

The Goose then told the Hummingbird how he had brought him water and protected him throughout the night. He promised to stay with the bird and help him until he was well again.

Even in his sickness the Hummingbird was surprised at the kindness of the other bird. He simply shook his head and whispered weakly, "Thank you."

Indeed, the Hummingbird was now grateful to be alive. When he had closed his eyes a few days before he thought for sure his life as a creature of the skies would soon be over, and he was ready to surrender to his thoughts of death.

Watching the great Goose hover above him the Hummingbird was confused and was not yet sure that death wouldn't still whisper in his ear again and call him away from the places he knew, loved, and missed with all of his heart.

Still unable to talk, the Hummingbird knew if he was going to live, he would have to trust this Goose. That thought frightened him more than his glimpse of death. All of his life it had been trust that had injured him more than anything, even more than the winds that had tumbled him and tossed him in this field.

"These brilliant colors of mine always kept people away from me," the tiny bird thought to himself. "Growing up alone, I was afraid to trust the other birds. Then my friend came into my life, I trusted her, fell in love, and my heart was broken."

The mental and physical pain of his thoughts and his broken body pressed in around the Hummingbird. Never, ever had he felt so helpless, so dependent on someone else, so confused about what to do. What should he do? What was there to live for anyway? Would he ever fly though the sky again, tasting the wind, watching the world below spin and sway as he let the currents carry him?

While the Hummingbird lay still again, thinking, lost in his uncertainty, the Goose knew that he had another serious decision to make and he was also lost in his own thoughts. The Goose flew off to bring the Hummingbird some more water, a little food, and to have a few moments alone to make his decision.

Before the Goose could ponder his own future, he heard the sounds of the flock returning and he was heartsick. The flapping and honking were getting closer each second. Caught there without a firm decision in his mind, he listened to the beating of his heart and hung his head.

What a picture the two distraught birds made. Both questioning their hearts, minds, and futures and both dependent, for different reasons, on the other for survival, both also groping for the right answer and the daring to do what they must, both alone except for each other. What would they do? What must they do?

4

ALONE IN THE wet field the Hummingbird also heard the other geese calling as they neared the creek, and a moment of terror gripped him from head to toe. The Goose had not said anything as he flew off and now, he was sure the big bird would not be coming back. It seemed as if his decision had been made for him, and if he were to survive he would have to find a way by himself.

The Hummingbird tested his body then, wanting to know if he could move at all—if he even dared to try. First, he moved his tiny feet. They worked. He could also move his right wing. He ached all over, but no matter how he tried he could not move his left wing. It was the left wing that had braced his fall, and he knew it would take weeks before he would be able to move it again.

Moving his legs and his good wing, the Hummingbird was able to push himself out of sight of the huge flock of geese. He felt certain that the Goose would not be returning now that the flock was back, and he was even more certain that another Goose might not treat him as kindly as the first Goose.

Guarded once again by the cornstalks, the Hummingbird lay back and wondered how he would ever find food and get water to keep himself alive while his wing healed.

Down by the creek, and still unaware of his gift from the Bird God, the Goose rose from the ground and flew to meet the other geese. He greeted the leaders and flew back to the ground with the birds as they began to eat and drink.

"Brother Goose, where have you been?" one of the leaders asked him. "We are ready to fly south, and we have been worried about you."

The leader stood by the Goose, waiting for an answer. For a moment, the Goose was terrified. The Goose hesitated for a second, thinking that he should perhaps just leave the bright-colored Hummingbird.   Maybe he should just fly south and forget what had happened.

But the Goose could not forget the little Hummingbird, just as he could not forget the other birds he had helped, and all the others he couldn't help. The whispers of the God were in his soul now. It was a strong feeling. A feeling that filled the Goose with the courage he had lacked before. The Goose listened, not to his head this time, but his heart, and he turned to talk with the leader.

"Sir, I have been helping a sick bird," the Goose said.

"What are you talking about? I have seen no sick bird," the leader replied.

"It is not a bird from this flock, sir. I have been helping a Hummingbird," the Goose said in a strong, clear voice.

"A WHAT?" said the leader, shouting so the other birds would turn to listen to this foolish Goose.

"You heard me, sir. I said a Hummingbird, and without my help he will die," the Goose said.

"This is ridiculous," the leader told him. "You must forget about this and prepare to fly with us at once. You have done many irresponsible things in your life but this, a Hummingbird, tops them all."

By now the other birds were gathered close, but the Goose, suddenly caught up in a decision he never realized he had made until that moment, did not even see them.

"I will not leave the bird out there, so it is better that you leave without me," the Goose said with nothing but certainty in his voice.

The other birds could not believe what they had just heard. No one had dared talk to the elder leaders this way. No one questioned an order. No one could believe the Goose would say such things and stay behind. It was unheard of and shocking.

Standing there surrounded by all the geese the Goose had never felt stronger. His head was high and his chest was ruffled out proudly. It was almost as if someone else had been speaking. He felt so sure of himself that he never waited for a reply from the elder bird.

"I will join you when I can," he told the leader, who stood looking at him in amazement.

"For years I have watched the weak birds, the sick birds in our own flock fall out of the sky, and never once was there a word said. Never once did anyone drop from the sky to help the bird. If that is how you feel, then I doubt you will miss one more bird on this flight."

The creek bed was filled with sudden silence. It was as if all the birds gathered around had quit breathing. No one dared to say a word.

The Goose seized that quiet moment. He bowed his head to the elder goose, jerked upwards, and with a huge honk he was circling above all the birds, watching dozens and dozens of heads pointed toward him. He dipped his wings, once, twice, and with those movements the flock of stunned birds disappeared from sight.

Oh, how happy the Goose felt! He could not believe what had just happened. Did he really say those things? For a while, he just circled in the sky, flying with abandon, reliving the past few moments. If he had been any lighter the big bird might never have touched the earth again. He felt so small, drifting there on the fall winds, and smiling with thoughts of what he finally had the courage to do.

It was there in that silent dark-blue sky that the Goose realized his prayer had been answered. He felt as if the Great Goose God was right there flying with him. The Goose offered another prayer of thanks for the courage and strength that he finally felt.

And the Great God was thankful that the Goose remembered him. He had known that someday the Goose could summon up the courage to do what his heart told him to. The Great God was proud, and he was with the Goose as the sky opened up into the warming sun of the afternoon. Soon the huge flock of geese could be seen dipping and swaying, a dark cloud of birds, moving south, quickly, swiftly and without looking back.

The Hummingbird saw that great v-shaped clump of birds and his heart sank even lower. The Goose must be with them and now he was alone again and with the thread of his life dangling so close to its end. Even though the afternoon air was beginning to warm him, the night's chill had left the Hummingbird unbelievably cold. He was also hungry, and his unquenchable thirst was again gnawing at him.

As he lay there covered with the remains of the fall corn harvest, he wondered why the Goose would be so kind and then abandon him. The Hummingbird thought about trust and he knew he should never have been tricked into thinking someone would help him. In his wondering and fear, the wounded bird once again felt his loneliness.

His desperation grew as he realized that without the help of the Goose he could not survive. The Hummingbird lay still and with the lack of movement his will to live came to an end again. He really did not want to see another sunset in this cornfield or another sunrise to warm him.

With his eyes closed to the reality that he was still alive, the Hummingbird couldn't see the Goose circling above him. He did not know what the Goose had just sacrificed for him. All he wanted was to be free of the life that he thought had brought him to this field and put him in such a place of helplessness.

Above him the Goose was lost. He could not find the Hummingbird anywhere. Finally, after flying up and down row after row of downed cornstalks, the Goose landed close to the spot where he had last left the Hummingbird. He walked back and forth, peering under cornstalks, until he saw the flame of color that could belong only to the tiny bird.

When the Goose peeled away the Hummingbird's corn cover the tiny bird was startled back to life.

"What are you doing?" the surprised Hummingbird asked. The Hummingbird could not believe that the Goose had come back now that he had willed himself to die.

"Go away and let me die in peace," he said to the Goose. After all he had just been through the Goose could only laugh at him.

"You are not going to die," the Goose said. "Now be still and trust me."

The Hummingbird could not believe the Goose wanted to be trusted after the thoughts that had just flashed through his mind. Why was the Goose there and not flying south with the rest of the flock?

For a while the Hummingbird wanted to fight back and order the Goose away from him. He was confused, afraid to trust, and so helpless.

But the Goose would not be scared away by the tiny bird. Nothing, it seemed, could make him want to leave.

"I am going to take care of you," the Goose told the Hummingbird. "I will bring you food and water and in a day or two you will be strong enough to be moved to a more sheltered area. I will not let you die."

The Goose sounded so confident and sure that the Hummingbird could no longer argue. Deep down inside there was a small part of the Hummingbird that longed to be free again. A part of him that wanted to feel the hot summer breezes gliding in across the brown desert plains. A part that wanted to see the cactus bloom. A part that wanted to see the white tops of the tall mountains shining in the morning sun. The Hummingbird was confused. He wanted to die. He wanted to live. He was afraid to trust. Afraid to share. He wanted to be free of all the pain, yet the efforts of survival alone, and without help, were more than he could bear.

The Goose went about his business as if the Hummingbird didn't have a thing to say about what would happen to him. The Goose was indeed determined to save the Hummingbird's life.

As he searched for food, the Goose could not help but feel a pang in his heart for all the birds that had left him behind. Dipping into his memory, the Goose could hear the other birds honking back and forth to each other as they headed south, the wind against them, the thought of day after day in the sky pressing against their minds.

"Where could they be now?" he asked himself. "Close to the great Horicon Marsh where there would be food and rest for days if the flock wished to stay that long? Or farther than that?" The bird wondered if they would miss him or if their honking laughter about what he was doing would carry them all the way to that night's resting spot.

The Goose would have been surprised if he really knew what the geese were saying and thinking. Talk in the flock was nothing but of the Goose who had stayed behind. As the flock increased in size, picking up new members here and there for the Great Fly, talk in the ever-darkening mass of birds grew louder and louder. The Goose and what he had dared to do was already an echo in the fall sky.

At first, when word of what had happened reached them, his parents were embarrassed and saddened. How could their own son go against the wishes and advice of the flock leaders? Ashamed, they melted into the large bird crowd and had never said good-bye to their son. Flying off with heavy hearts, wondering if they would ever see him again, something was beginning to stir within their breasts as they listened to the other birds.

"You know he has always had a kind spirit, and we have always laughed at him," said one bird flying in the great migrating flock. "Once when I was sick, he helped me land safely and later all I could do was laugh at him. How I wish now that I had his courage, that I could be like him."

Other birds up and down the long, v-shaped lines were saying the same things, and by the first nightfall not a bird went to rest without worrying how the Goose would make it through the change of the seasons.

As the days passed and the birds grew closer and closer to their winter home, the Goose was fast becoming a legend. The parents of the Goose began noticing that the other birds were kinder and watched for them in a soft, quiet way— the way their own son might care for them. This Great Fly would indeed be a trip to remember. It was more than a changing of the season, they said, it was a changing of the heart.

But hundreds of miles away the Goose didn't know what was happening with his family and friends. As his own days passed, he barely had time to think about the birds that had flown south.

The Goose's day was consumed with taking care of the Hummingbird. The small bird needed food and water, and the Goose had so many things to sort out in his mind. As the days passed it seemed to get colder and colder, and every morning the frost from the night before stayed longer and longer.

Even though the Goose was now totally devoted to the tiny bird, the Hummingbird still found it hard to completely trust him. He had totally surrendered the care of his fragile body to the Goose, but he could not let the bird inside his mind and heart. He seldom spoke to the big Goose, but he studied him carefully.

He noticed the Goose was larger than most of the other Geese he had seen and when the Goose took off to find more water or food, the Hummingbird was stunned by his graceful movements.

"This is no ordinary bird," the Hummingbird said to himself. "He is large, he is strong. Truly he must be a leader. So why is he helping me?"

That is a question the Hummingbird could not answer. He wondered about it over and over in his mind until one morning he simply blurted it out while the Goose was standing close.

"Where are the rest of the birds?" he asked the kind Goose. "Why do you take care of me like this when you don't have to, when we are not even birds of the same flock?"

"The other birds are heading south," the Goose told him. "And do we not both have wings and feathers, and hearts and souls, and are we not now talking in the same bird language?"

The Hummingbird could not disagree, and it was his food for thought for many days to come.

That conversation somehow began drawing the two birds closer together, and the Hummingbird began the slow process of trusting the huge bird that was carefully nursing him back to life. They began talking about their families and friends. They shared remembrances of places they had been and even bragged about flying feats until finally one day the Hummingbird dared to tell the story of his lost love.

As the bond between the Goose and Hummingbird grew stronger so did the Hummingbird. But even as the bond tightened and the birds knew they were friends, the snow started to fall and the Goose knew it would take more, much more, than just trust and

friendship to get out of the cold, winter winds
to a place of safety, survival and life.

5

ABOUT TWO WEEKS after the geese had headed south, the Goose noticed a more than drastic change in the colors of the sky, a change he had never seen before. Usually when the winter winds blew into the cornfield with all the power and fierceness of a champion season, the Goose was long gone.

When he saw the dark clouds getting closer and closer, and the air circling in great white sheets, the Goose instinctively knew that by the next day the snow would be deep. For a short time that sudden knowledge paralyzed the big bird.

He was no fool. He had known all along that sooner or later he would have to figure out what to do with himself and with his tiny friend. Feeding the Hummingbird and nursing him back to health was one thing but surviving in the cornfield throughout the bitter winter months was something else. It might be possible for the Goose to wait out the winter, but a small, sickly, fragile bird might not make it to the spring season.

The Goose still had a hundred questions to settle in his mind. He had just barely gained the trust of his small friend and now he must come up with the solution to the biggest problem he had ever faced.

The Hummingbird had slowly been getting stronger and stronger, but the Goose knew the bird would not yet be strong enough to fly. He would never be strong enough to buck the early winter winds, and survival in the fields throughout the cold, long, harsh winter months was impossible for them both.

The Goose's mind was racing with questions as he prepared for the snowstorm that was already dropping tiny, light flakes of snow onto the cold ground. There had been a few storms during the past two weeks but nothing close to what the big Goose knew he would see this day and night.

He quickly gathered up enough food for both of them for several days. The bird made dozens of trips back and forth across the fields to gather up food, and then spent a long time pushing some pine boughs and corn stalks into a small shelter.

The Goose worked quietly thinking about what lay ahead. He knew that soon the winds would be blowing across the fields and without a secure shelter both he and the Hummingbird would perish.

By the time the fierce wind shifted, and the snow started pounding down from the sky to the still-dark earth, the Goose had finished the shelter and was ready for the hours, or days he would have to spend huddled beneath the stalks.

The Goose pulled the tiny Hummingbird in close and began the long wait. A part of him was grateful for the storm. He needed time to think about the huge problem that faced him and time to come up with some kind of plan, some kind of idea that would save not just one life, but two.

The Hummingbird was not used to the snow. He dozed on and off throughout that first cold and very snow day. He never knew if his dreams were a part of reality or his reality a dream. In his most fitful sleep, he remembered over and over again his terrifying ride through the sky. His dreams of the fall from the sky always ended with a loud cry but then he was comforted to feel the warmth of the Goose over him.

The two birds talked on and off during those hours and days in the shelter. They shared the events, feelings, places and people that had filled up the spaces of their lives. Sometimes they talked about silly things. They talked about growing up and what had led them to this predicament where they were huddled in a serious fight for life in circumstances that sometimes seemed terrifying.

When the little bird would fall off onto one of his fitful sleeps the Goose would spend his time searching for an answer to his terrible dilemma. He searched deep inside himself for some clue, some notion, some instinct of survival that would get him and the Hummingbird through the harsh winter months. The harder he looked, the harder he thought, the more he knew there was no answer. He felt as if he was doomed and fell asleep that night with tears in his eyes and thoughts of failure in his heart.

The snow continued to pelt against the cornstalks and filled up the field with inch after inch of fluffy white snow.

When it finally stopped, fall had been overrun by winter, and all the sights, scents, and feelings of that now-old season were gone.

It seemed as if the entire earth were still. When the snow stopped, the wind stopped with it, and everything that had been alive before seemed dormant, as if it had been covered in a huge blanket and was now sleeping.

By now, all the other birds were safe in their winter home. They had seen the dark sky to the north and felt a chill from the arctic storm. They wondered if and how the Goose had lasted through the first phase of winter. The mighty winter winds had helped push them faster than expected to the warmth of another field and place.

The Goose knew when the storm quieted that for now the worst was over and yet he dared not open his eyes. He was still without the answer he needed, and he desperately needed an answer soon if there was to be another season of life for him and the Hummingbird.

The Hummingbird spoke first, and his words were not easy for the great Goose to hear.

"We must leave soon," the Hummingbird said. "The winds and snow have stopped, but they will both come back. We must go now and quickly if we are to stay ahead of the next storm."

The Goose was quiet at first, wondering what, if anything, there was left to say.

"You cannot fly," he finally said. "And I will not leave you. We will have to stay."

The Hummingbird knew that it was likely that least one of them would not live if they stayed in the fields much longer. He knew also what a risk the Goose had taken to stay, and he knew something even more important, something the Goose did not know.

The tiny bird moved away from the Goose and told him this story.

"Tiny birds have many strengths. But there are so many times also when our speed and our daring cannot match the strengths of the bigger birds," the Hummingbird said, barely moving as he spoke.

"Because of our limitations we have taught ourselves to be careful. We have learned to watch out for the winds, the change of light on the water, and the warnings the skies often shout to us. Our fathers and mothers teach us to be wise, and they show us many things that even birds like you do not know. They teach us words of wisdom that have been handed down from generation to generation and from Hummingbird to Hummingbird.

"Long, long ago the tiny birds of the sky discovered a way to ride across the heavens without using an ounce of energy, without moving a single muscle, a single wing. That is how both of us will leave here, together," said the Hummingbird.

The Goose was stunned. He thought his friend was delirious and that he had taken a turn for the worse and was ill again. He could not believe the fantastic story the Hummingbird had just told him. He had no idea what the bird had been talking about.

"What are you saying?" the wide-eyed Goose asked the Hummingbird.

"Turn around and I will show you," ordered the Hummingbird.

The Goose did what he was told. The Hummingbird told him to open his wings as far as he could. He pushed back the small shelter and both birds were immediately standing in the open.

"There have been many times when small birds have had to do this to survive," said the Hummingbird. "They usually do this without many of the big birds even knowing what is going on."

The Goose was still mystified. He did not have a clue about what the Hummingbird was about to do.

At that moment the Hummingbird pushed himself in back of the huge wings of the Goose and disappeared from sight.

The surprised Goose did not even feel the presence of the Hummingbird behind his wing. The small bird burrowed in deep and nestled in a spot that seemed to have been carved out to fit his exact shape and size.

"I can ride behind your wing without you even noticing it," the Hummingbird said. "This is the answer to our prayers."

The idea was so simple and so wonderful the Goose could hardly believe it. Why didn't he know about this? Why had no one ever told him?

The large Goose bowed his head and silently thanked the Great Goose God for the answer and for one more chance.

It was late afternoon when the Hummingbird again tucked himself under the Goose's wing. Both birds knew that even a few hours of flight into the early evening would bring them closer to safety and survival.

Once the tiny bird was under his wing, the Goose rose quickly into the sky, almost forgetting his small passenger, and circled around the field once more before leaving.

He tipped his wings to the farmer, not knowing if the farmer would even notice the lone bird in the sky, and headed south across the snow-white field.

The air up high was cold, and the Goose knew the flight south for him and the Hummingbird would not be easy. But the Goose also remembered other flights south. He remembered all the times he wanted to help other birds and didn't. He remembered what it felt like to know something in your heart and to act against it.

Behind him the sky was darkening in across the empty field, and the Goose flew hard and fast to put as many miles between him and winter as he could.

The big bird's wings moved up and down as he glided through the chilly air watching for familiar landmarks and concentrating on his flight.

Underneath him the Hummingbird was warm and secure. The little bird had no idea where he was going. He knew he was alive and that he was with a true friend, and for the moment that was all that really mattered.

Off they flew across the sky, barely anticipating the next day's adventures, not knowing what would happen, or where they were headed.

The two birds truly became one on the flight. Racing the season across the sky and feeling a bond of friendship that had already saved one life and rescued another.

The journey south was easier than either of the birds expected. The Goose seemed to surge through the sky with some hidden source of energy, and each mile brought with it warmer and warmer temperatures.

Behind the two birds the sky became the dark, shallow, moody sky of winter. Light filled up the sky later and later each day, and nighttime seemed to gobble up the remaining light of the day just moments after the sun had risen.

For the Hummingbird the ride was exciting. He could rest throughout the day and into the evening as the Goose flapped his big wings back and forth, honk, honk, honking with a feeling of immense happiness. The tiny bird's wing was healing rapidly and soon the Hummingbird would be able to fly himself.

The Goose hadn't made a conscious decision to fly to his usual watering place, but that is where he was headed. He instinctively knew the way and followed all the familiar signs and the path became very clear to him. The Goose was heading back to his family, his roots, the places and experiences that had helped form his life, and to the things that had brought him to this time and place.

It would be just a day, maybe two at the most, and the Goose would be at the same wintering spot as the rest of the flock. It was a thought that was in his mind, and his heart was beginning to become uneasy.

6

THE HUGE GOOSE seemed tireless to the small, fragile Hummingbird. He wondered time and time again what would have happened to him if the Goose had not helped him. Surely, he would have been dead by now. He wondered, too, where the Goose was headed and what directions both their lives would now take.

Minutes turned into hours and hours into days as the pair raced across the wide sky. The nights were warmer and warmer and the tiny bird felt better each day.

One night when the birds had stopped to rest, the Hummingbird turned to the Goose and asked, "Where are we going?"

"I am not sure," said the Goose. "I have just been flying the same way I have always flown but I am frightened about returning."

The Goose told the Hummingbird how the birds taunted him and how he wasn't sure if he would be accepted back into the flock.

"We should go back to the place you know," said the Hummingbird. "Perhaps the birds have had a change of heart."

The Goose was silent. He was remembering how difficult it was to turn from his leader and to stay and help the Hummingbird. He remembered every detail of the harsh scene.

"I am afraid," he admitted to the Hummingbird. "Afraid of what the other birds might say to me and what they might say to you."

The Hummingbird was still unaccustomed to his new feelings of sharing. For a moment, he was quiet. He wasn't exactly sure what to say to his friend. After a time, he spoke softly, looking into the eyes of the big, sad Goose.

"My friend, you have already taken the risk and won," said the Hummingbird. "You have flown through the skies and you have been true to yourself and true to the feelings in your heart and soul. Now nothing can ever be the same again. There is nothing to do now but to go home," said the tiny bird. "We must go to the place you know."

When he finished, the Hummingbird wondered who had been talking. His newfound thoughts, his own feelings of caring and sharing with the Goose, almost startled him.

"You are right," said the Goose. "We will fly on and we will take what is given to us. At least I will have you there with me and that will make it easier."

With that said, both birds knew the risks that lay ahead. The winds of the sky had suddenly become calm and friendly, but the winds of life might not be so kind.

7

BACK IN THE desert country those who knew the Hummingbird had given up all hope of ever seeing him again. Stories about what happened to him circulated through the area and his family was prepared to deal with the grief of missing someone they loved.

During the quiet days and nights that filled up the Hummingbird's life now, he often thought of all those he had left behind. He wished there were some way to let them know he was safe and that he was being taken care of.

He also had a lot of time to compare himself to the bird he once had been. There were times when some of his thoughts shamed him. Times when he remembered how he had used his beauty to impress the other birds. Times when he remembered how he had dismissed the words of caring from the other birds when his love had disappeared from his life. He often wished, as he flew under the big Goose's wing, that he could go back and have a second chance at love, friendship, and life.

The Goose had his own thoughts, his own regrets, as he commanded his body through the warm winds. He wondered what he would say when he saw his family and friends again. How he wished he could take back some of the strong words he had said to the elders! How he hoped he hadn't shamed them and his beloved family!

Even though the Goose knew in his heart what he had done was right, he knew also that there could be hard times ahead and that he still might have to fight for what he believed was true and right. With those thoughts, the two birds continued to grow closer and closer to the wintering spot of the geese.

8

THE GOOSE WAS soon able to smell the moist scents of the warm earth beneath him and it seemed as if each day the sun was growing larger and larger.

They seldom met other birds on their fly. They had been so late in getting out of the cornfield that other birds had long since arrived at their winter homes. Many times, it seemed as if the two birds were the only air animals alive. They wondered if they were the last two birds left on the face of the earth.

The Goose had no way of knowing how many days he had been flying, but one bright morning he recognized the sweet smell of the sea and knew that suddenly he was within miles of the flock.

He circled an open field before moving his big wings in circles and dropping to the earth.

"We are almost there," he told the Hummingbird, "and I am frightened."

The Hummingbird thought how strange it was to have the huge bird say such things. He had just flown hundreds of miles and risked his life to save a tiny bird and yet he was afraid.

"My friend, I do not know what to tell you to make this easier for you," said the Hummingbird. "I know you have saved my life, and without you I would not be here. I know that you are good and kind and strong.

"Already your courage has shown itself, and now there is no choice. There is nothing to do but turn ahead and face what happens," said the Hummingbird. "The decision has already been made."

The Goose remembered then how he had prayed to the Great Goose God. He remembered the total feelings of helplessness and the deep feelings in his heart and soul that pushed him to do the things he never thought possible.

"You are right," said the Goose. "The decision has been made. It is time to go on."

The Hummingbird tucked himself up under the big wing for the last time and felt again the great surge of strength that powered the two birds back into the sky.

The Goose pushed on, feeling the coolness of the ocean air surround him as he grew closer to the water. He wasn't sure where the birds would be nesting. It could be anywhere along this stretch of coast and so the bird headed north.

He flew on for a mile or two, glad to be close to the water, intent on a final destination. Suddenly he turned south again. Instinct took over and the Goose flew toward a little remembered piece of swampland, inland perhaps, five miles from this Northern stretch of coastline. After flying for less than a mile the Goose spotted a group of Geese flying toward him, and he knew he had found what he was looking for.

When the flock of geese heading toward the coast first spotted the lone Goose, they did not recognize him. They were surprised to see a goose all alone and were even more surprised that the Goose didn't fly away from them.

As the birds pushed closer the Goose strained to recognize one of them. He did and called out, honking as they all flew together. When the other geese recognized the Goose they immediately circled back and dipped under him. They could not believe their eyes.

"Where have you come from and how did you get here?" they called after him, flying quickly to be closer.

The Goose was surprised at the friendly greeting and as the other birds talked to him, he knew all his past fears were for nothing.

The Goose had become a hero without even knowing it. The birds continued circling around and around him and asked him what seemed like a million questions, while the Hummingbird lay still, and quiet, listening in disbelief.

The Goose was just as disbelieving. He was shocked by the genuine concern from the other birds.

"What had happened to all the birds that had lashed out at him as he helped the other birds?" The Goose wondered to himself as he looked around him in shock.

The Goose moved on to where the flock of Geese had congregated. He flew over the dark mass of birds and wondered what could possibly happen next.

He finally landed at the edge of the great flock. Smoothing his large wings behind him, he searched through the crowd for the familiar faces of his parents. The Hummingbird continued to lay still under his friend's wing, terrified, not knowing what to do.

A great crowd was gathering around the Goose and walking up through the center of the crowd was the leader of the geese. Ahead of the leader the Goose finally recognized his own family, and he felt his heart move within his huge chest.

The Goose hesitated for a moment, still unsure of his final welcome, and then he rushed to greet his parents.

The reunion was wonderful, and the Goose forgot about everything for a few moments as his parents surrounded him.

Finally, the leader of the flock stepped up to greet him. "Welcome back my friend," said the leader. "You have been missed and we have worried about you and prayed for your safe return."

"Sir," stammered the Goose, "you know that I stayed behind to help the Hummingbird, and he is here with me now. We came here because this is all I know, this is where my flock comes, this is where my family winters."

"Where is your friend?" asked the leader. "I don't see him anywhere."

"Come out little Hummingbird," the Goose said to the tiny bird.

The Hummingbird slowly tumbled out from behind the Goose's wing. When he hit the ground there was a gasp from the other birds. "Where did he come from?" they all asked.

"He rode here, tucked under my wing," said the Goose. "Look under your own wings and you will see a place small enough for a tiny bird."

The other birds were astonished to see that a bird could fit under their wings. The Hummingbird then moved in and out of a dozen wings, showing the big birds where he had ridden with the Goose. It was a comical sight to see the birds jumping up and down with excitement when the Hummingbird fit into their wings.

While the Hummingbird was wing hopping, the leader of the geese took the Goose aside and talked with him slowly and softly.

"At first when you told me what you were going to do, I was angry and disappointed," said the leader. "I kept thinking that you would leave and be close behind the flock.

"But time passed and you never showed up," he said. "Soon I began to listen to the other birds talk about all the times they had wanted to help other birds but were overcome with fear.

"I began to remember old feelings that I had put aside," the leader told the Goose. "I began to remember all the birds who had dropped from the sky that might now be with us if someone had helped."

The Goose was listening in stunned silence. He wanted to tell the leader he understood, but the leader went on.

"One night all this remembering, all this thinking of what we had not done, made me realize that I had been mistaken," confessed the leader. "I knew you were right and that we had been wrong."

The leader said by the time he had realized his mistake the flock was too far south to turn back for the Goose. But when the flock reached the coast, word had been passed that something amazing was going to happen.

"When we arrived here, I gathered everyone together and told them my feelings," said the leader. "I said that we had a duty to help not only the birds in our own flock but all the birds in the sky."

The Goose was astonished. He couldn't believe what he was hearing.

"I do not know why we have been so cruel and why it has taken us so long to do what is right, but I thank you for having the courage to do what is right and set an example for all of us."

Then it was time for the Goose to speak.

"Sir," said the Goose, "I don't know what to say. I am no hero but a simple bird who listened to the cries in his own heart and did what he had to do."

The Goose had no real knowledge of the gift from the Great Goose God and so what he said to the leader he said with true honesty.

There was silence then as the two birds stood close, looking at each other and feeling a bond of understanding come between them— a bond that would last throughout dozens of stormy seasons.

9

THE MONTHS FOLLOWING the homecoming of the Goose and his tiny friend were filled with many adventures. The days were warm and long, and the Hummingbird traveled up and down the coast with the Goose, exploring a part of the world he had never seen before.

His wing healed perfectly and soon it was hard for the Hummingbird to remember the dismal day he spiraled through the sky and lay near death in the unfamiliar field.

The Goose was busy when he wasn't flying with the Hummingbird, showing the other birds how to fly low, spot, and then help tired or ill birds. He worked with most of the birds, telling them what to watch for in weak birds, and how to make them stronger.

The Hummingbird felt welcome and loved with the Goose and his flock, but he had a feeling of sadness that never seemed to leave him.

He missed his family terribly. He wanted them to know he was safe. He wanted to sail through his old skies and near the sides of the huge mountains.

The Hummingbird wanted to laugh with his friends and share with them in ways he had never done before. The Hummingbird was homesick and he knew with each passing day that soon he must leave the flock and search for his own beginnings.

1 0

WHEN THE WEATHER in the South turned warmer than usual and the sun beat down day after day, the Hummingbird knew a change of season had come and gone. He also knew it was time for him to leave the Goose and all of his other friends.

When the flock began to prepare for the fly back north, the Hummingbird was wondering how he would find his way back home, and how he would tell the Goose he must leave.

The Hummingbird never got the chance to look for the Goose because the Goose sought him out first.

"I know you must leave," the Goose told him one day. "The thought makes my heart heavy, but I know well the pains of missing, and you must find your family."

The Goose and the Hummingbird talked and remembered. They discussed the first moments of their meeting, the fears of sharing and trusting, and remembered the ride through winter back to summer.

"Thank you for giving me the chance to do what I needed to do," the Goose told his little friend. "I will never forget these moments and the friendship you have given me."

The Hummingbird said it was his vanity that caused the meeting. He said he would no longer be a bird that was a loner. He said he wanted to travel through the skies—not alone, but with the feelings of a bird that had triumphed over himself and his weaknesses.

"Your courage and daring have shown me the true meaning of those words," said the Hummingbird. "My heart is full and ready to learn, grow, and share, and it is all because of you."

The night before the Hummingbird was to leave the flock prepared a huge feast. The Hummingbird dared not sleep, for in the morning he would say good-bye to his dear friend, and he knew the parting would be very hard.

But the morning did come, as mornings always do, and it was time for the Hummingbird to set out on a new journey.

He left the flock quietly and headed west in the direction the Goose had pointed out for him. He was filled with a depth of sadness that had only been surpassed by the feelings he had when his love had left him. He wanted to cry out into the wind and turn back.

Suddenly the Goose appeared next to him. The Hummingbird was startled and then filled with happiness.

"I wanted to say good-bye one last time," the Goose told him. "And I wanted to tell you one more thing...something very important."

The two birds sailed slowly through the sky for a moment, one so large and one so small, a startling difference against the morning sky.

"My heart also aches at your parting my friend," the Goose said. "What you must know is that love and friendship do not end in the parting."

The Goose told the Hummingbird that the two birds could always be together in their minds and hearts. He told the tiny bird that whenever the Hummingbird felt a cool breeze riffle through his wings it would be a message of fondness and love from the Goose.

"There will not be a day that I do not remember you and what we have shared," said the Goose. "You will live on in my memory and in my heart forever and whenever a Goose helps another tiny bird a part of us will be there also.""

Then the Goose moved away silently, and he was but a blur when the Hummingbird circled to see him one last time. He saw the bird's huge wings making the same majestic movements that had once carried him to safety. In a moment the Goose was out of sight and the Hummingbird moved on alone.

11

THE HUMMINGBIRD EVENTUALLY made his way back to his family and friends. His story of survival and his own change of heart endeared him to all the birds he met. The seasons passed and soon the Hummingbird had his own family. The tale of his adventure with the Goose was passed down through the years.

Not a day went by that the Hummingbird didn't search the sky for the familiar sight of the big Goose dipping in across the horizon. When the seasons changed, the Hummingbird would become quiet for days, remembering the one season that had changed his life, remembering a Goose that taught him the true meaning of love, friendship, sacrifice, and life itself.

The memories kept him warm, and on days when he floated through the skies alone, he would drift through the currents, suspended between today and yesterday, never feeling lonely because his heart was full. Because he knew the Goose was with him, dipping under the clouds, and always watching for a helpless bird.